Princess Nayrobi M

Written by TK Jones

You are Wonderfully Made

Copyright (c) 2022 TK Jones
All rights are reserved. No parts of this book may be reproduced without permission from the author or publisher except as permitted by U.S. copyright law
For information reach out to
tanayjones92@yahoo.com

Once upon a time, there was a small kingdom in Africa ruled by King Niguel. The King and his Queen Aija had a beautiful daughter called Nayrobi. She was a princess if there ever was one. She loved experiencing new things.

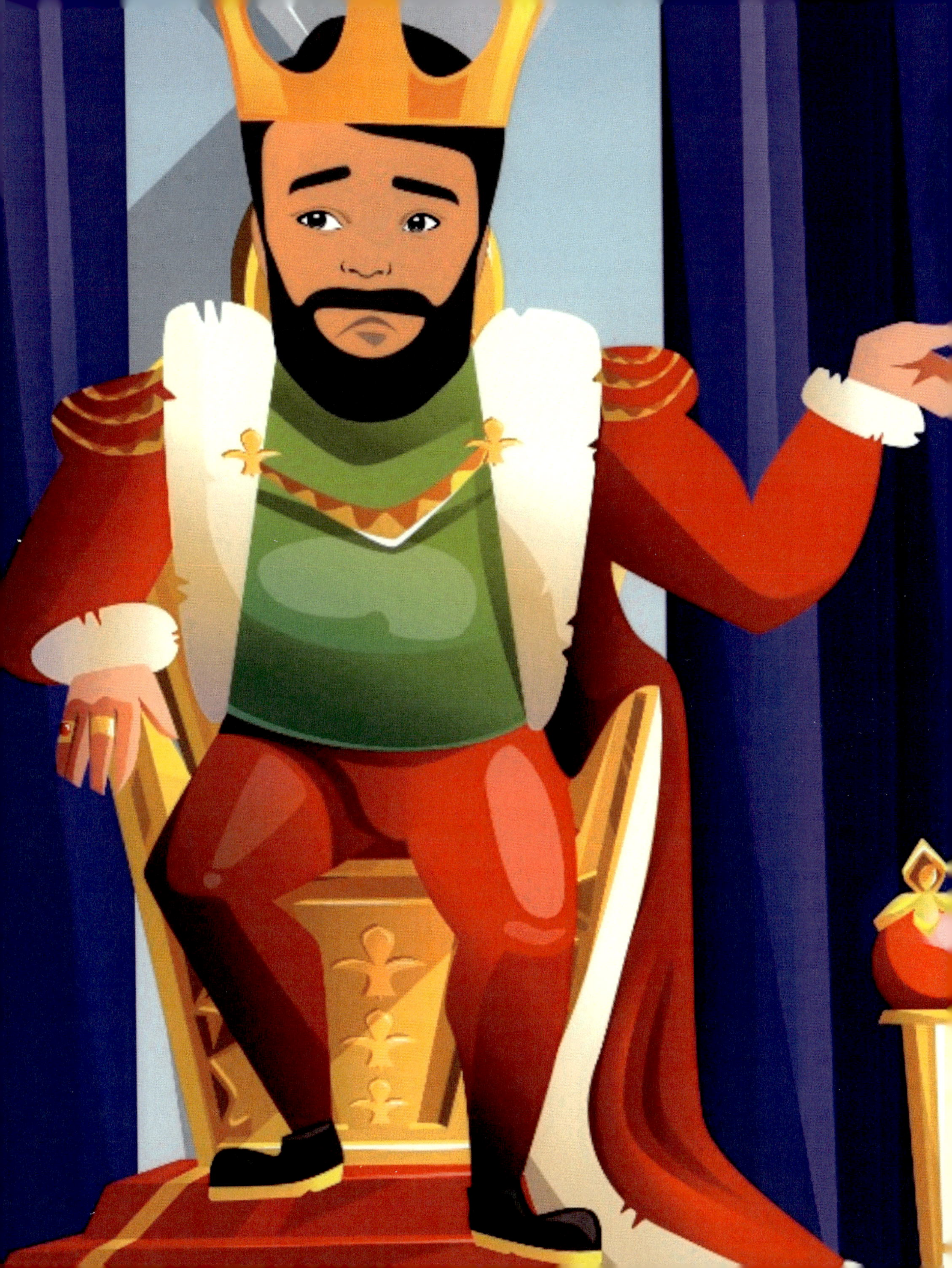

She was always eager to watch her father conduct the legal duties for their kingdom. She would watch as the citizens of the village would come in to discuss matters with The King. Sometimes they would bring their children, who seemed so happy and friendly to the Princess.

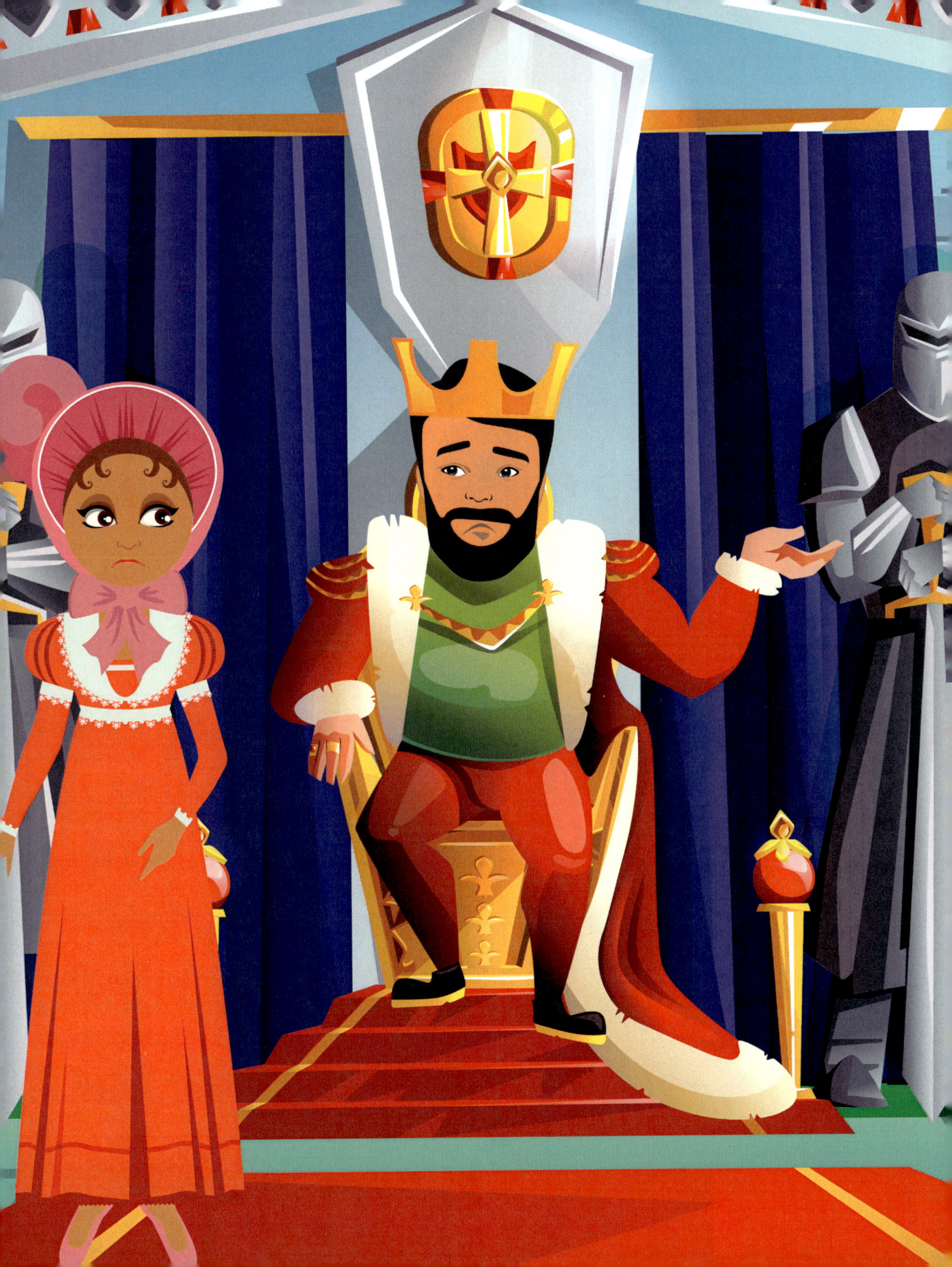

As Nayrobi watched the children play in the courtyard, she thought to herself, I wish I could play with them. It's not fair that I only get to play with children when we visit other kingdoms. Nayrobi felt sad because she was not allowed to play with the children in her village.

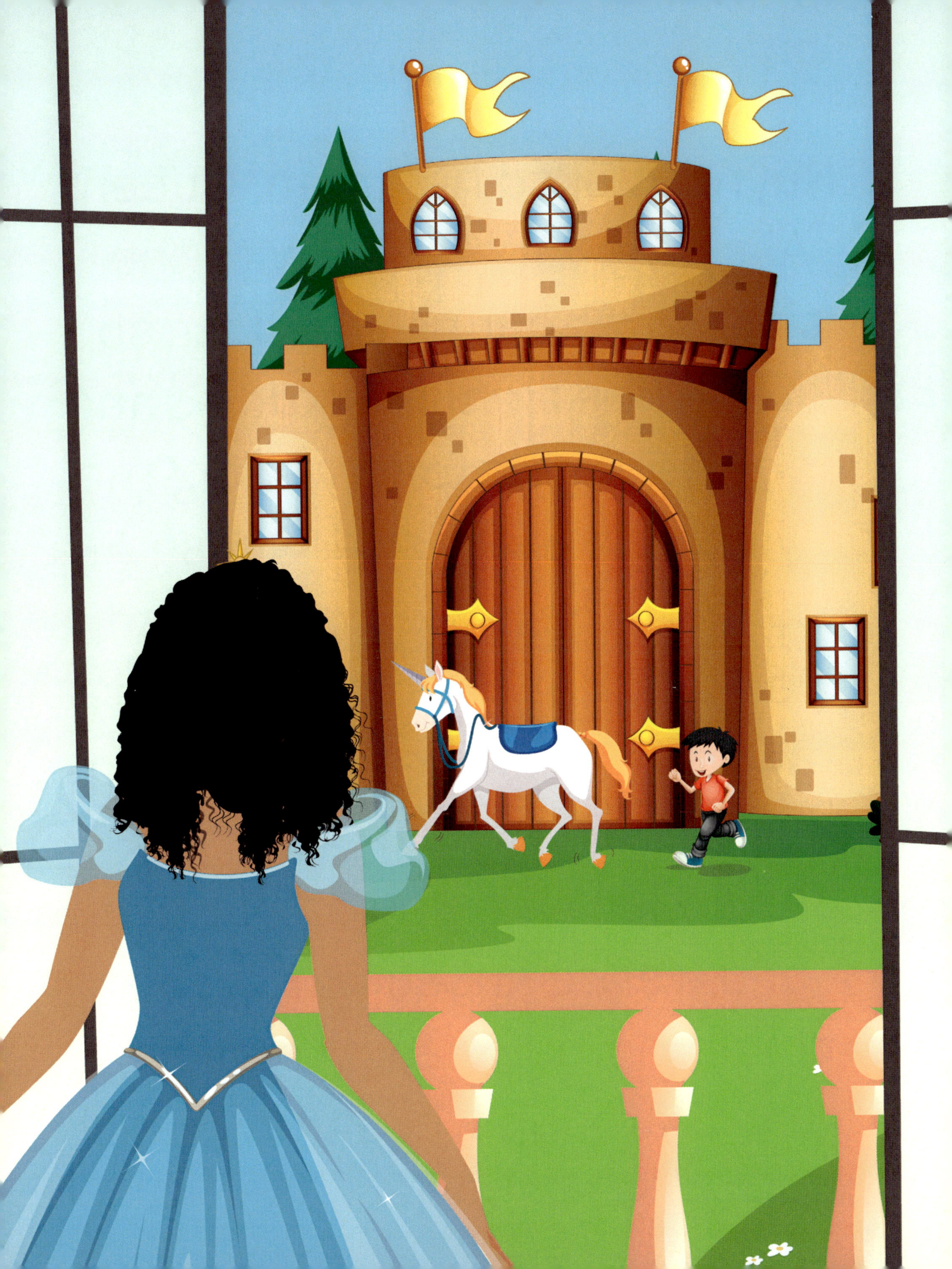

Nayrobi asked her mom, Queen Aija, why can't I play with the children in our village? I am so bored aside from my studies and hobbies. It gets lonely being the only child in the castle. Queen Aija explained, there are many reasons you may not understand right now, but one of the main reasons is your safety. You must have protection with you at all times and we are not sure how the children would react to having guards around while they play.

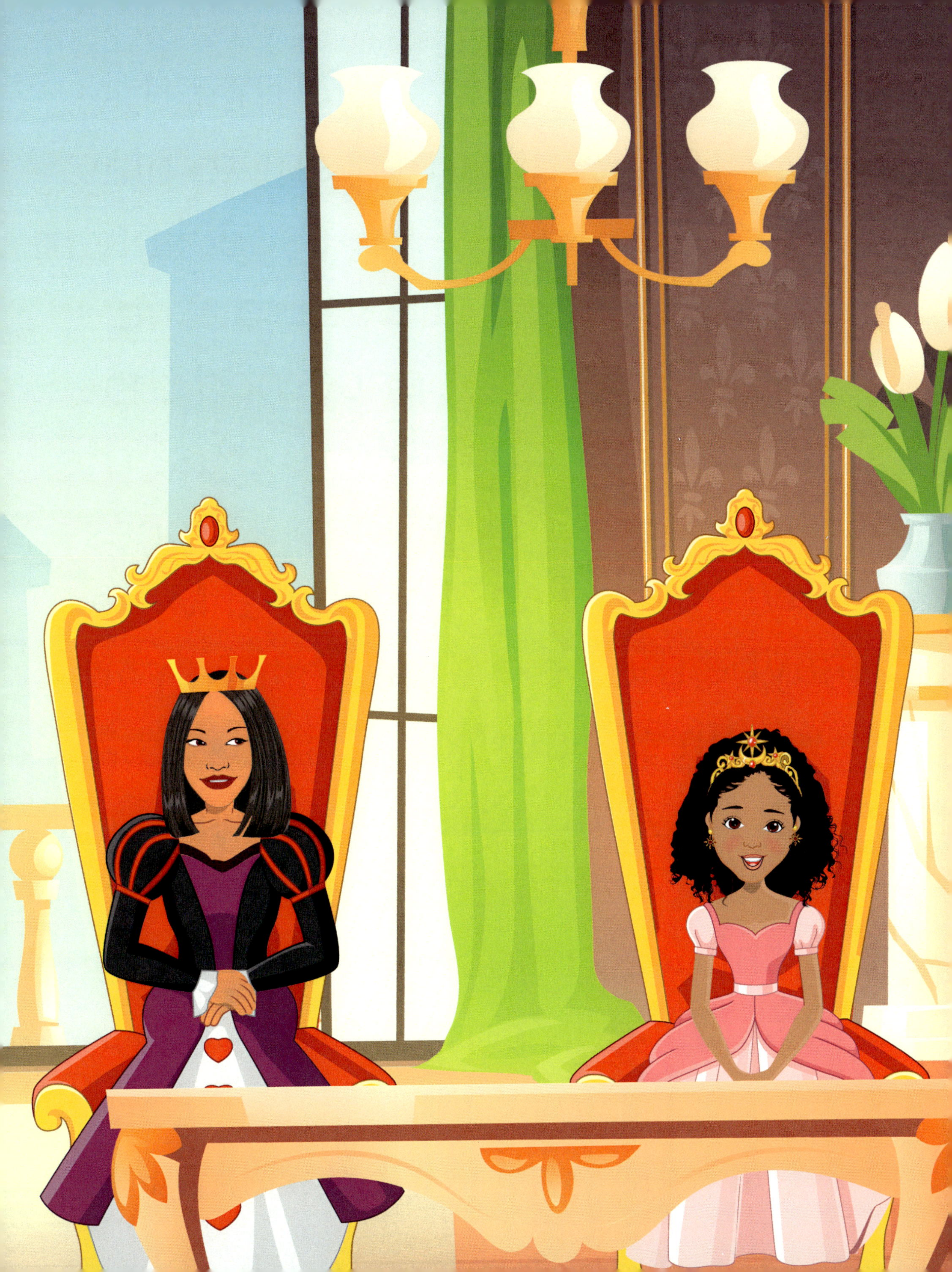

The Queen was afraid that the children would not want to play with Princess Nayrobi, especially in the presence of a guard. The Queen was also concerned that they wouldn't be able to trust the children she befriended. Princess Nayrobi had another idea. Mom, maybe the next time children are within the castle's courtyard I could play with them then, said the Princess. The queen thought about the children rejecting the princess and said, I don't think that's a good idea right now, but I will discuss the idea with your dad later

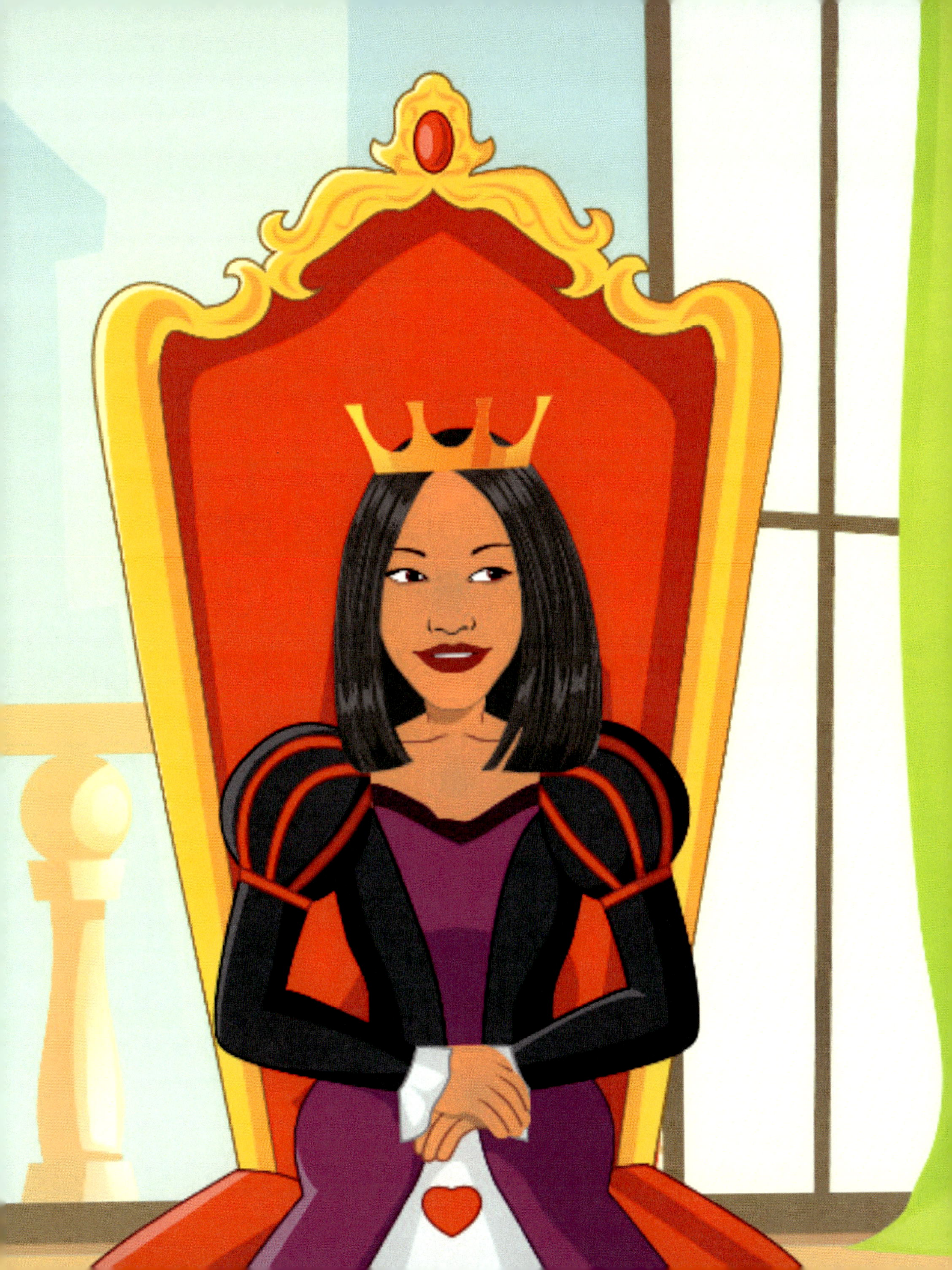

Princess Nayrobi thought to herself. The next time children are within the castle walls I will disguise myself so I can play with them.

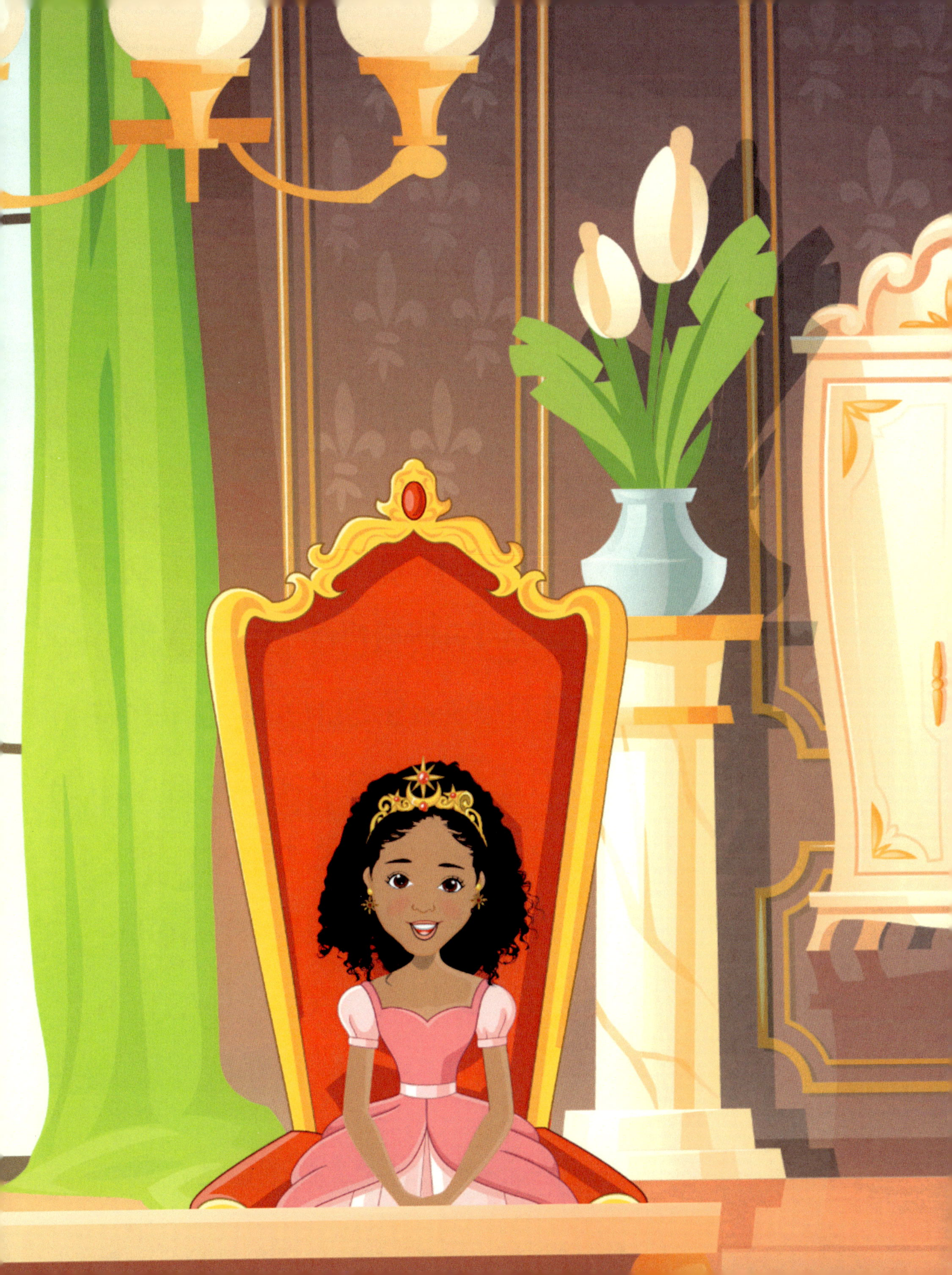

The princess did just that. The following week there was a group of children in the courtyard; more than usual. The Princess thought now was my chance. She put her hair up in a ponytail and put on her gardening clothes as she did when she was working in the garden with her mom. The Princess thought I could play with the children now as she sneaked into the courtyard.

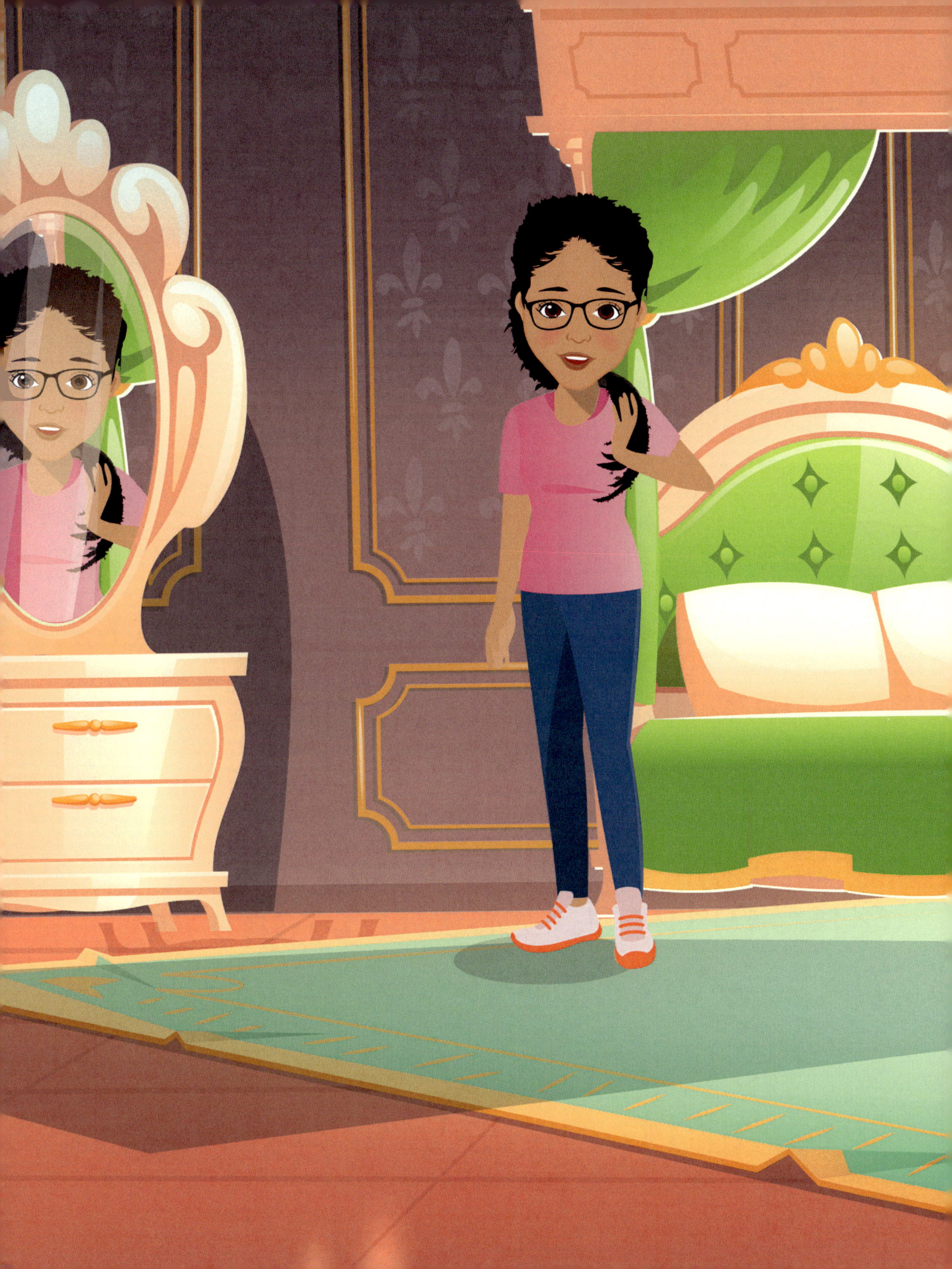

As Princess Nayrobi walked toward the children she thought what will I say? She didn't have time to think long before the young boy that ran past her tagged her saying "you're it." She immediately began to chase him and the other children. They ran and laughed as they waited for their parents to meet with the King. Just as the boy that tagged the princess said, "Time out, I'm tired. Let's rest for a while." He saw his parents come out of the castle, so the boy and his sister ran toward them waving goodbye.

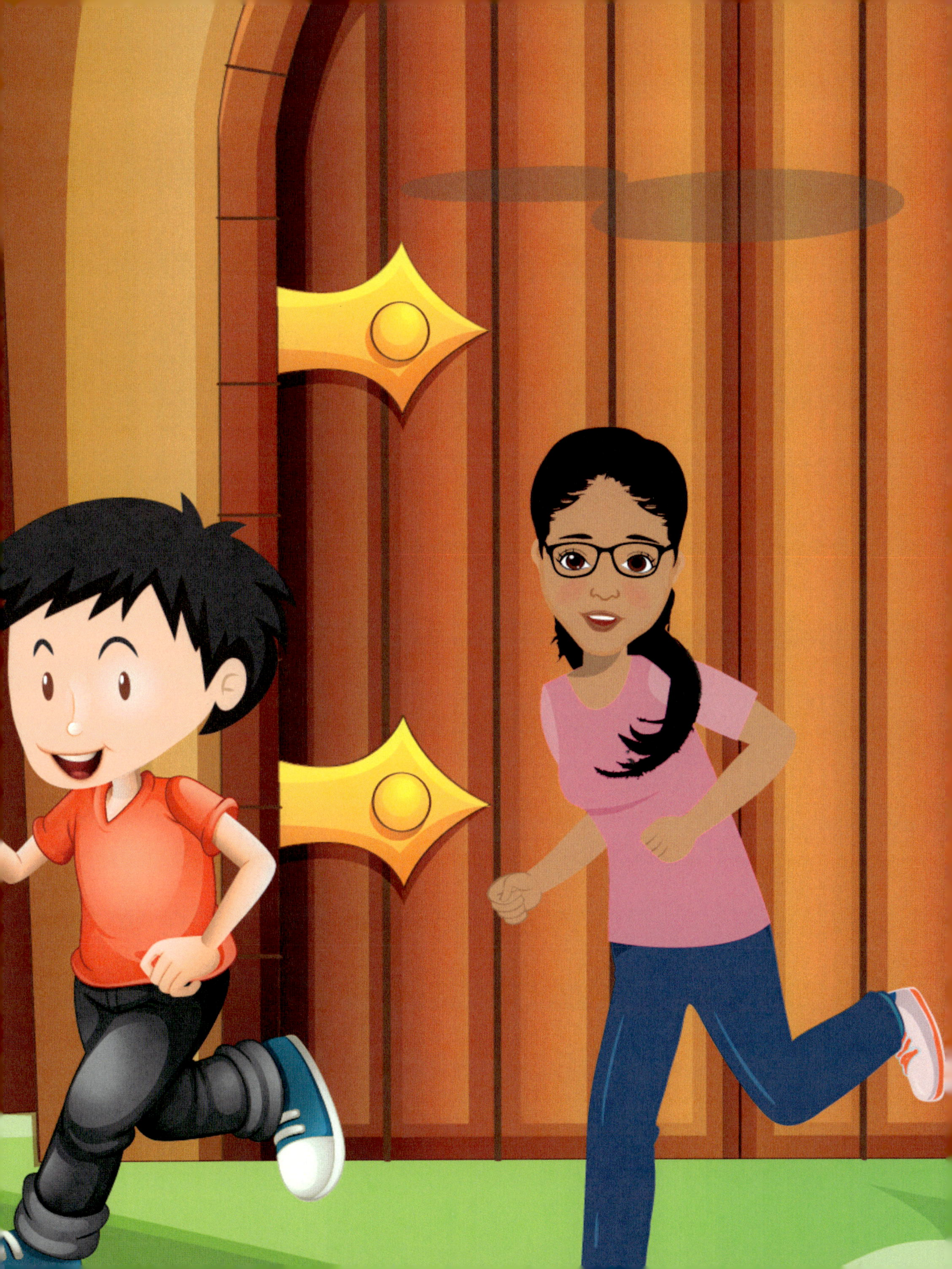

As the two children left, one of the girls said hi I'm Amandi and this is my sister Amani. What's your name? My friends call me Bee said Princess Nayrobi. Well said Amani then that's what we will call you Bee. Amani let's go there's mom said Amandi. Hopefully, we will see you next time Bee, Goodbye. The princess said goodbye as she waved. She was so happy she was able to play with the children today that she lost track of the time.

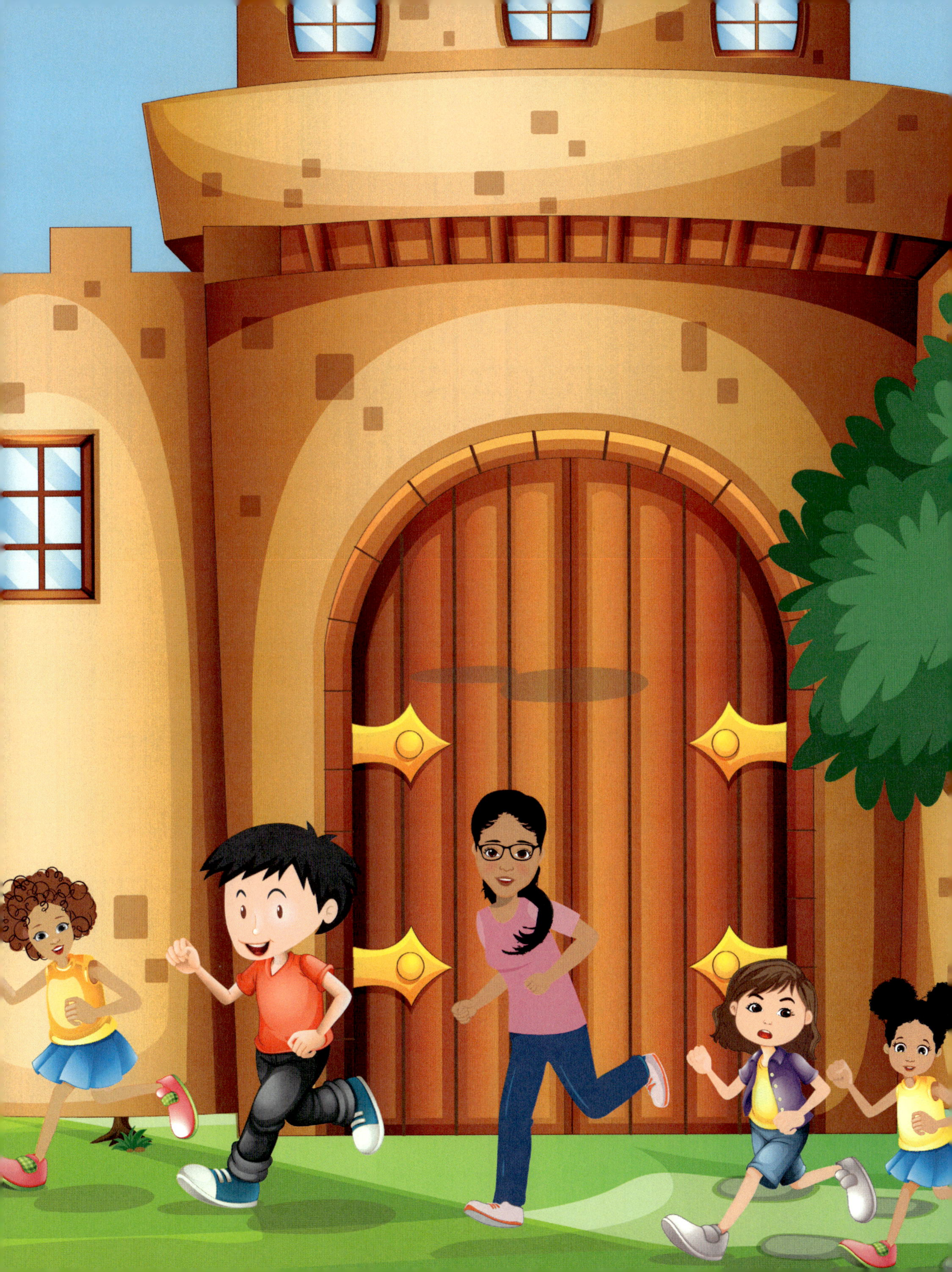

Nayrobi heard her mom calling her so she ran into the garden to pretend she was working on the garden." Oh, there you are. I was looking all over for you. It's time for your History lesson. Get cleaned up, and report to the study please." said The Queen. "thanks mom, I will." said The Princess. Then she went and did as she was told.

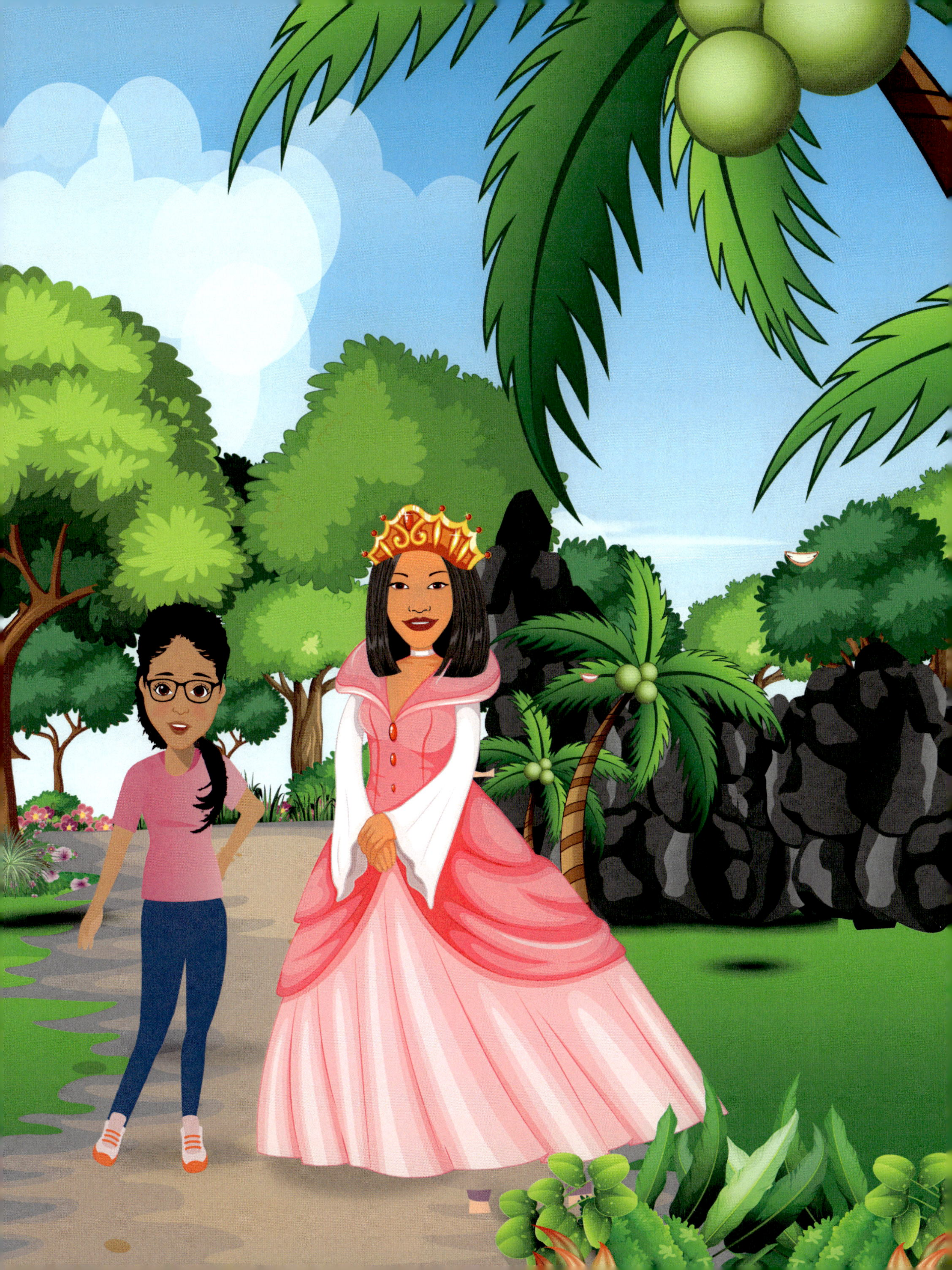

After her history lesson, it was time for dinner. She was so tired She could barely eat her food. The princess could not wait to go to bed. She had a long fun day and was ready to get some sleep.

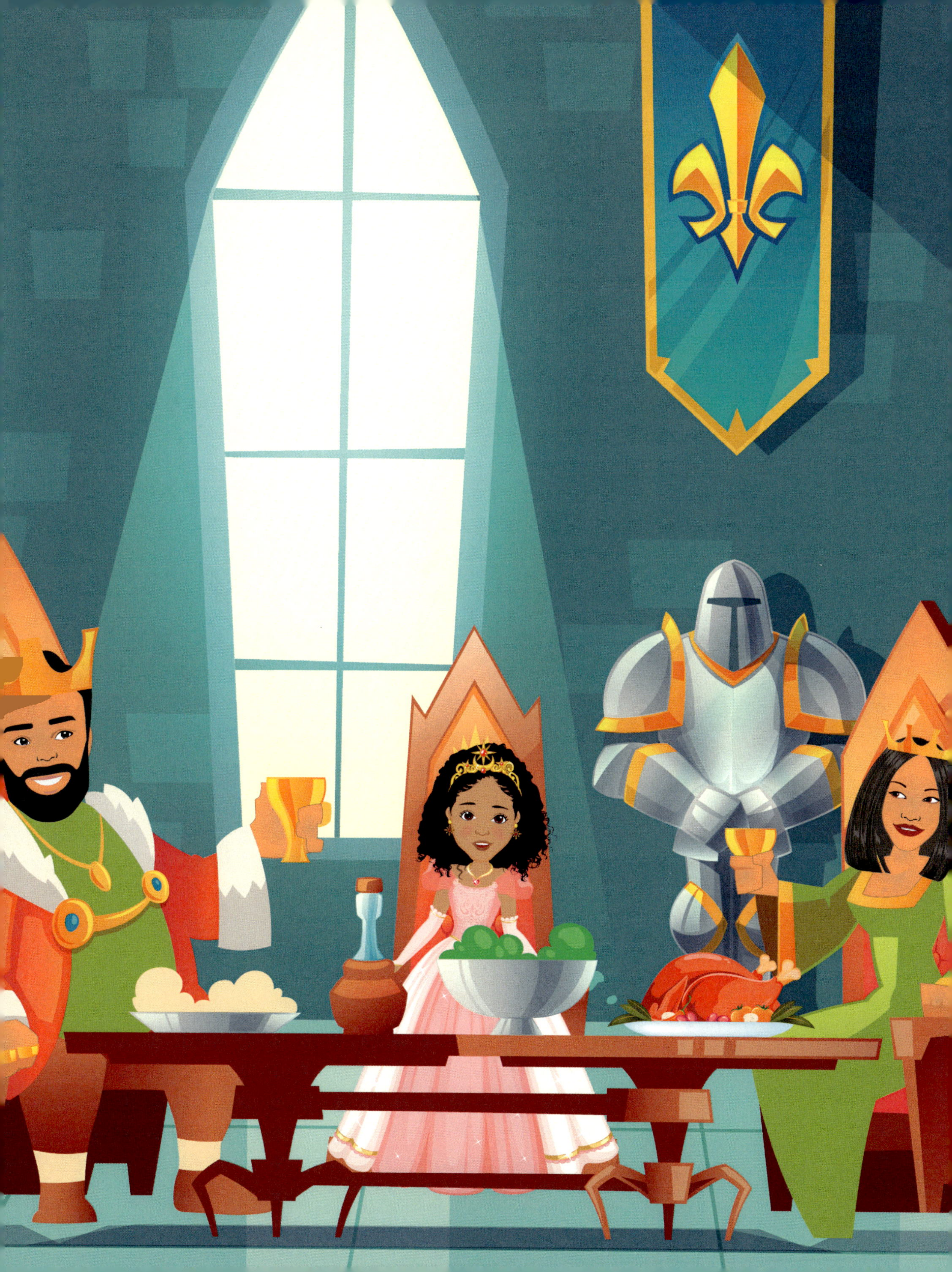

The next day the princess completed her normal routine for the day, occasionally checking for children in the courtyard. Several days passed and still, there were no children playing in the courtyard. The weekend came and went.

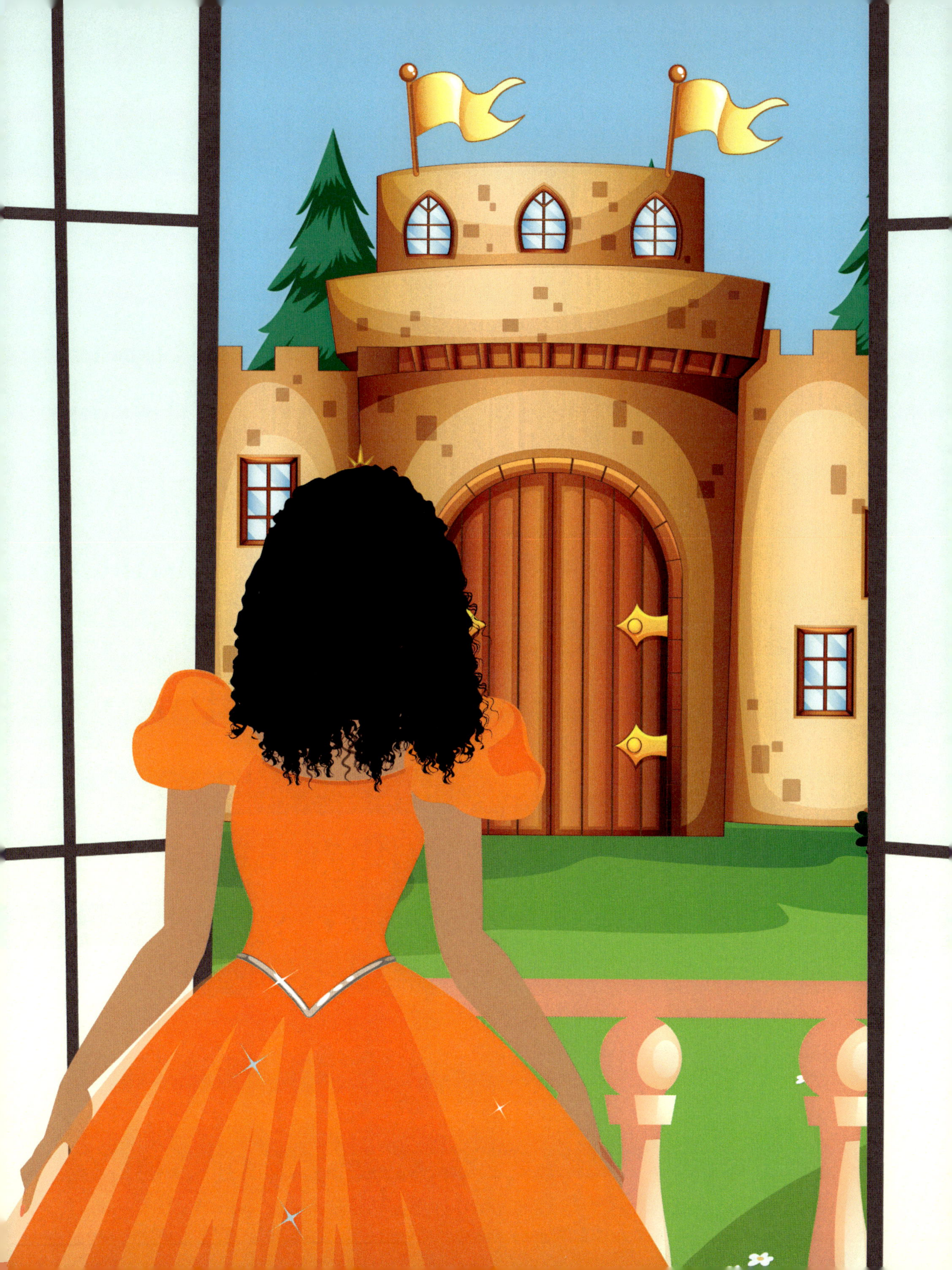

Finally, today is Monday, said the princess. Hopefully, soon children will show up today. When the princess checked the courtyard she saw Amandi and Amani playing a hand game in the courtyard. The princess changed into her garden disguise and joined the girls in the courtyard.

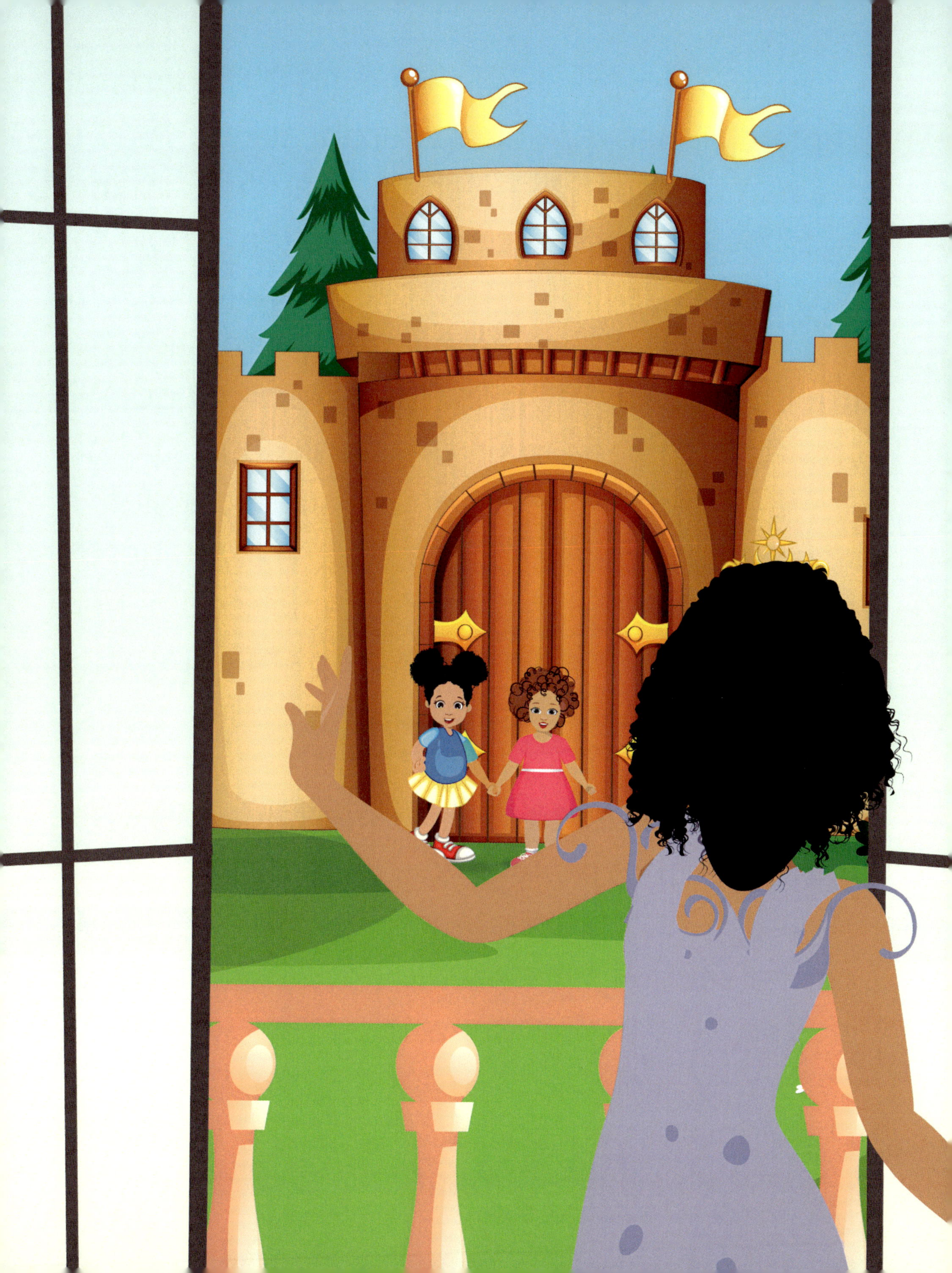

Hi said the princess to the girls. The girls replied Hi Bee. Princess Nairobi asked, what's the name of that game you're playing? Amandi said "numbers." Do you want to learn how to play it? Yes, I would love to learn, said Nairobi. They began to teach Nayrobi how to play the numbers game. The princess asked Amandi Will you guys be back again this week? She said no, we only come on a Monday since our dad supplies the eggs for the king. Are you here every Monday too? asked Armani. Yes, I'm here every day because my dad helps maintain the kingdom. Wow said Amandi every day, so do you ever see the princess? Before the princess could answer. Amani said sometimes I wish she would come to say hi to us even if she can't play with us. The girls were so involved in their conversation that they did not see their mom. Let's go, said their mom with an odd look on her face. Bye see you next Monday, said the girls. The Princess sensed that their mom knew who she was, but couldn't be sure.

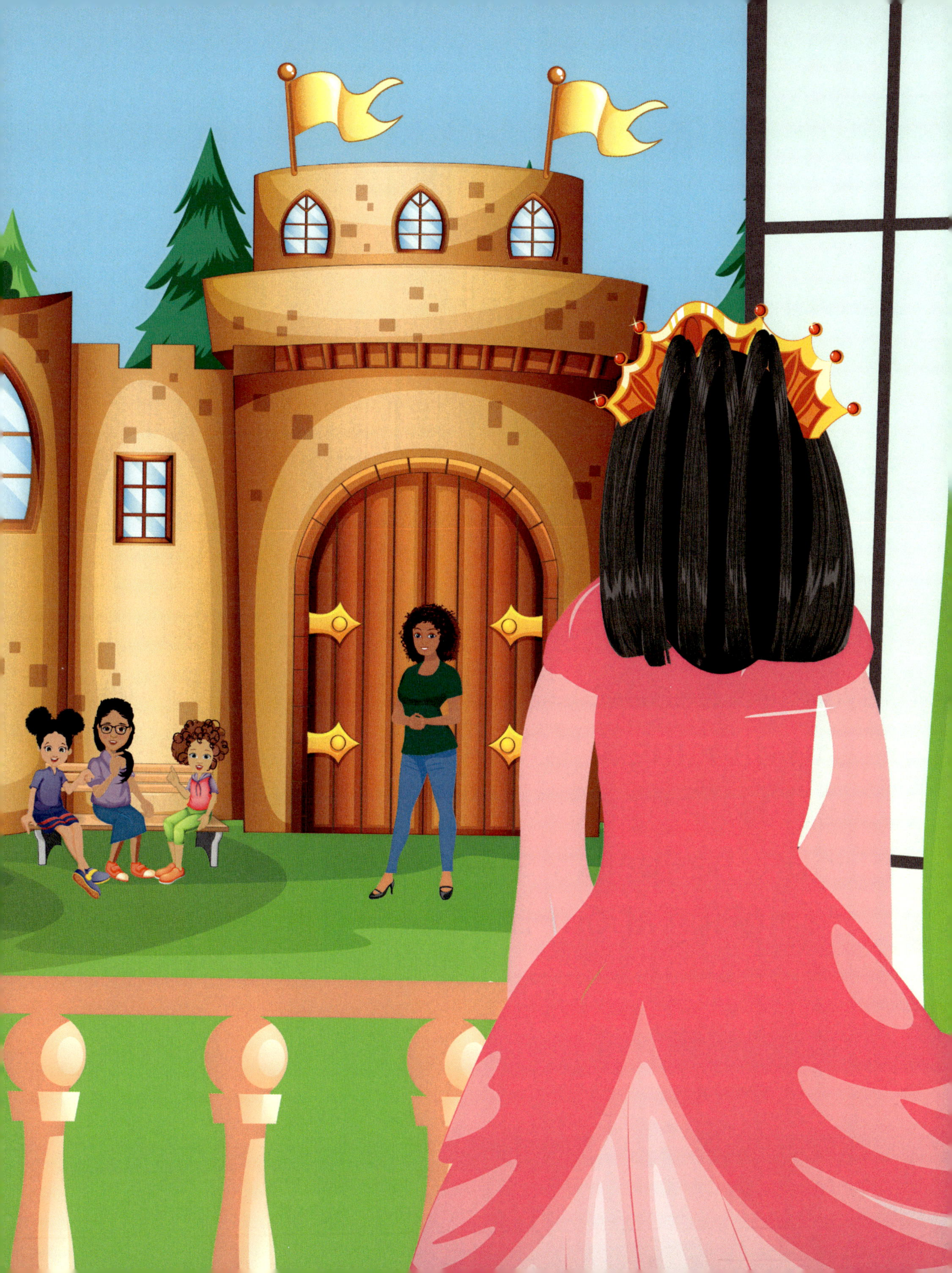

Several weeks had passed since the princess began playing with the children

One night while having dinner, King Niguel said "Nayrobi, mommy, and I are having a party this weekend to honor some of our village merchants." "That's great, daddy. I love it when people visit the castle. Food, music, and dancing; it will be marvelous," said the princess. After dinner the princess said good night to her parents, and went to bed, excited, thinking about the party this weekend.

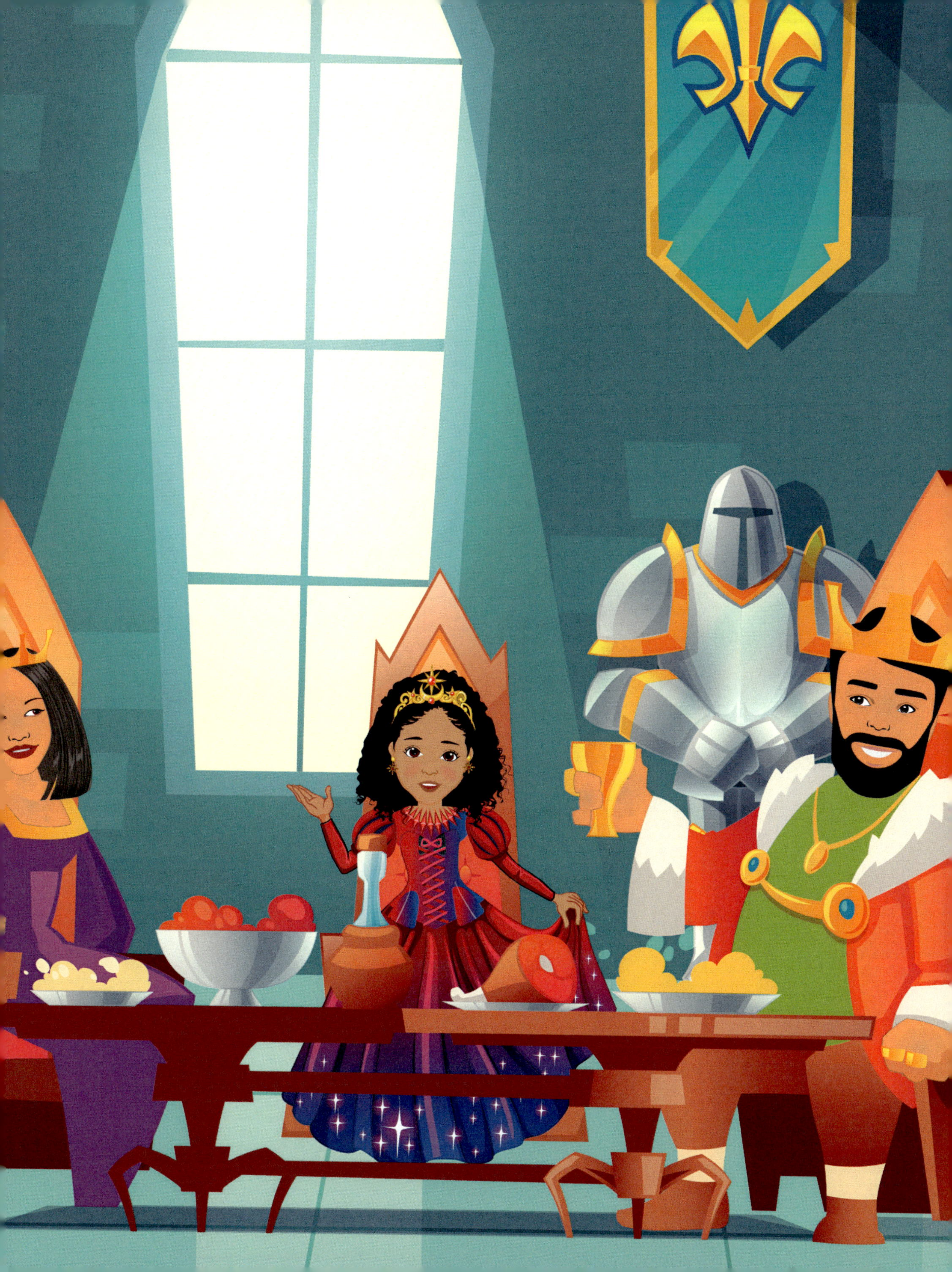

The party day had finally arrived. The princess had her breakfast that morning and rushed to prepare for the party. Even though she was used to being the only child at the celebration parties, she didn't mind because the castle seems to come alive when filled with people. She couldn't wait to hear the music and see people dancing. The guest had already begun to arrive so the Queen called out, Nayrobi we have a surprise for you. I'm coming mom, the princess replied.

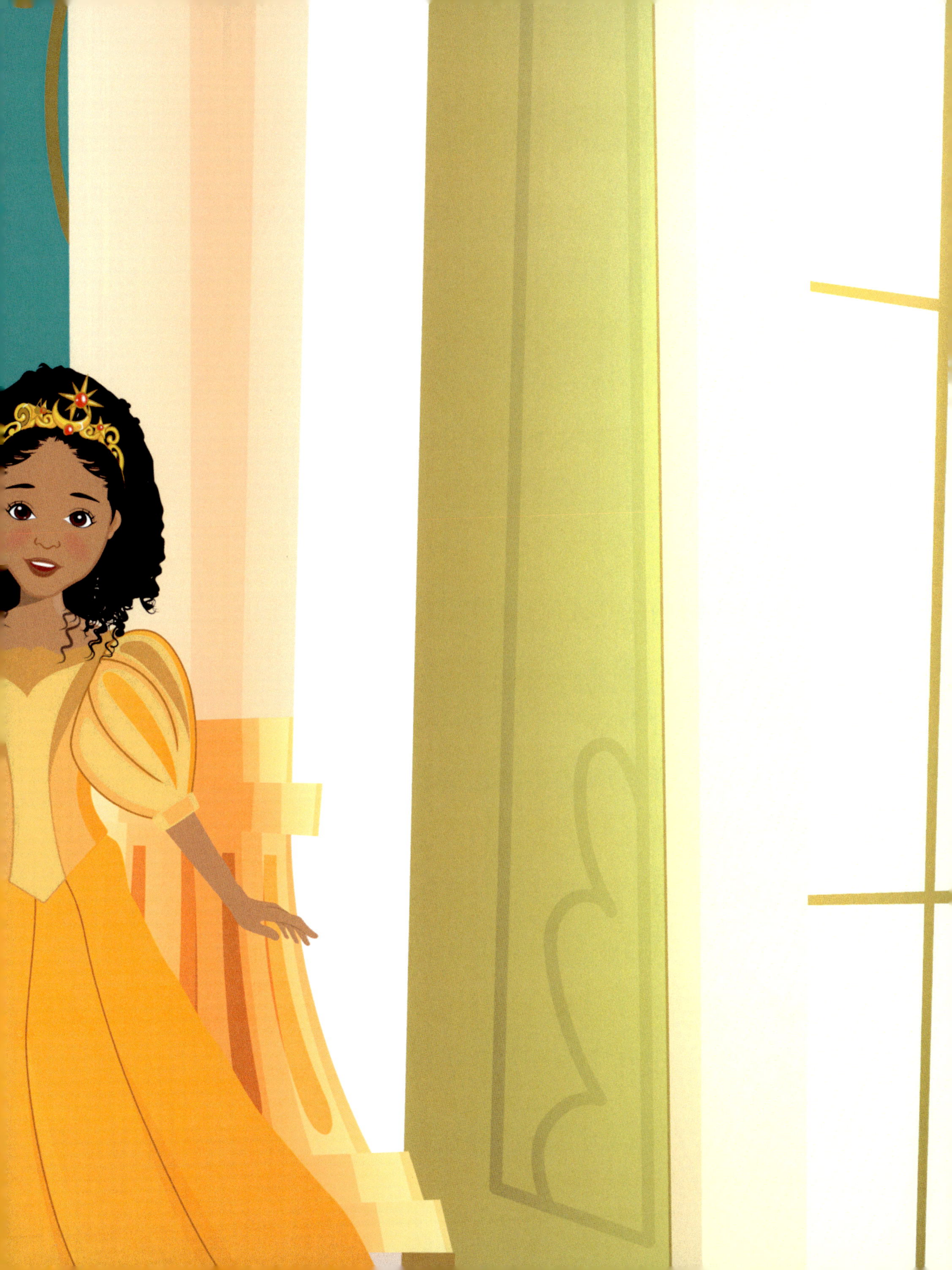

When the princess arrived in the ballroom, she saw the children. The Queen introduced the children. Nayrobi was surprised by the presence of Amandi and Amani that she didn't hear the names of the other children. The princess could see that the sisters recognized her and were preoccupied with how they would react now that they knew she was the princess. After the introduction, the princess approached Amandi and Amani saying it was a pleasure to see you again. Amani was so happy to know she had been playing with the princess, but Amandi was upset because she felt deceived. So after greeting the princess all of the children surrounded the princess except Amandi. Amandi went to sit on the other side of the room by herself.

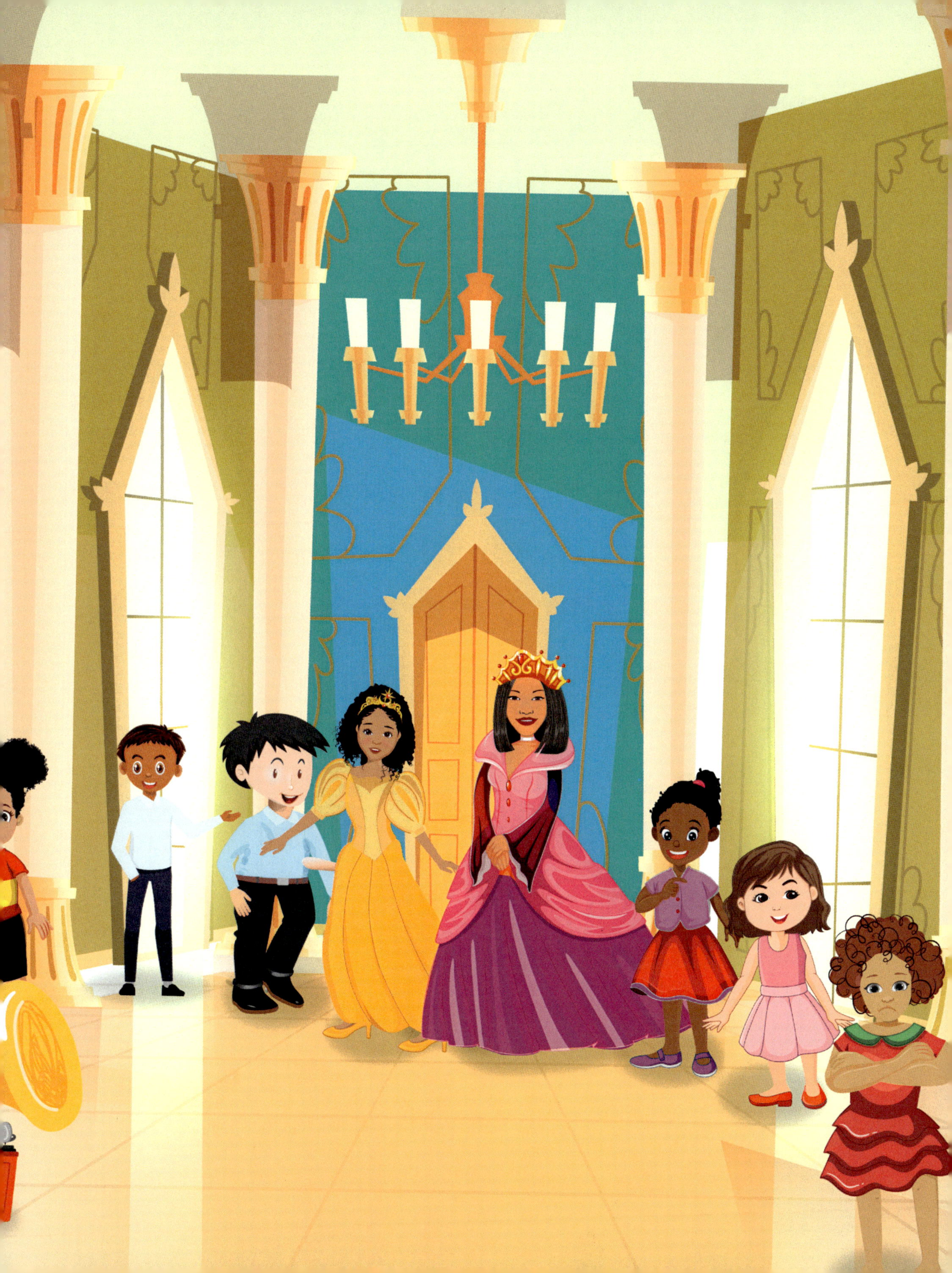

When princess Nayrobi got the chance she went over to talk to Amandi. The princess said. "I'm sorry Amandi. I should have told you the truth about who I was from the very beginning and I understand if you don't want to be my friend anymore. I just hope you will forgive me one day because I really would like for us to remain friends."

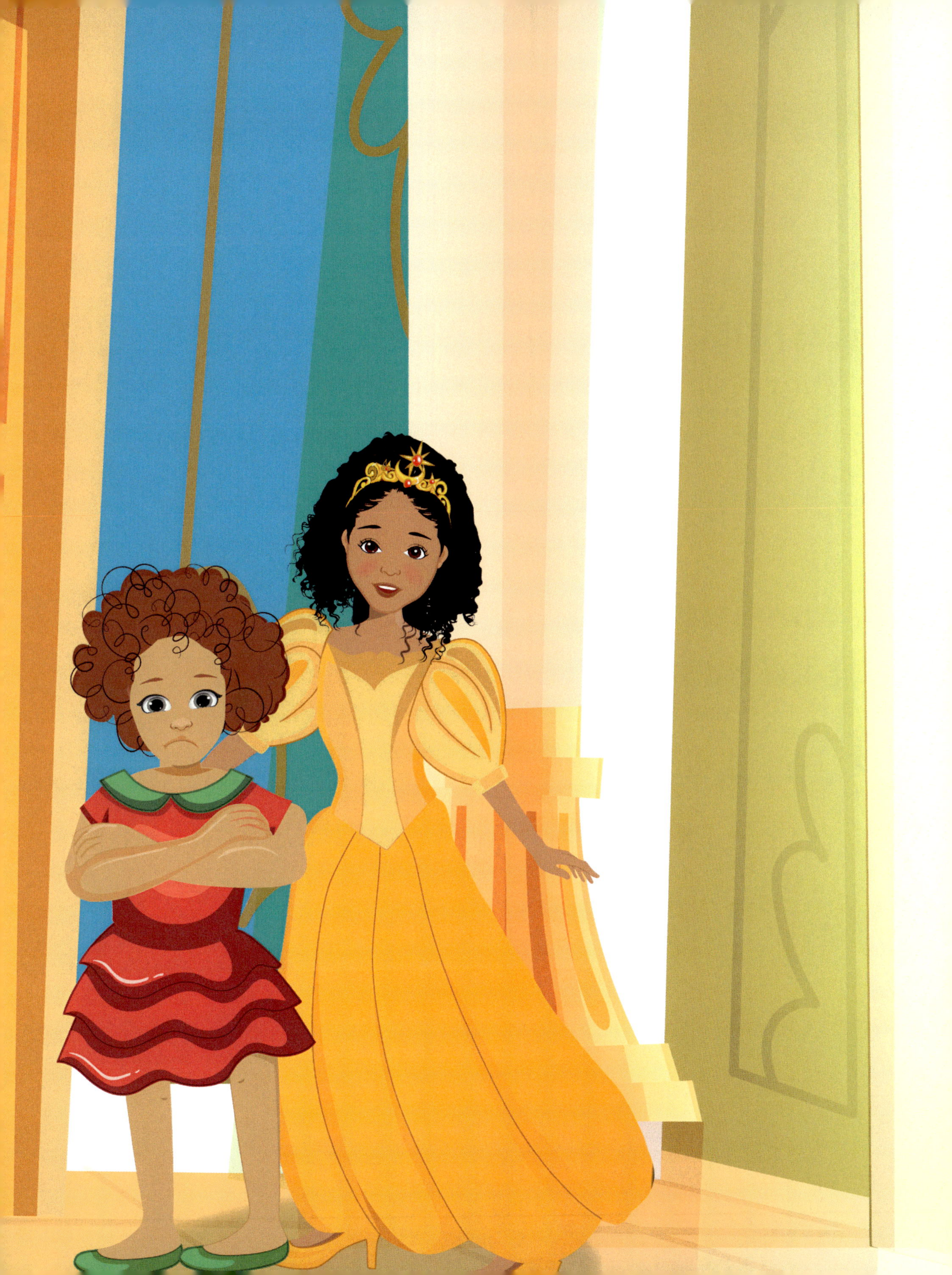

The princess joined the other children who were on the floor dancing. Shortly after that Amandi also joined the group of dancing children. The Princess was glad to see that Amandi was dancing and having fun. As the party came to an end Amandi told Nayrobi that she forgave her for not being truthful and that she would be glad to continue being her friend. The princess replied Thank you, Amandi and I'm honored to have you as my friend.

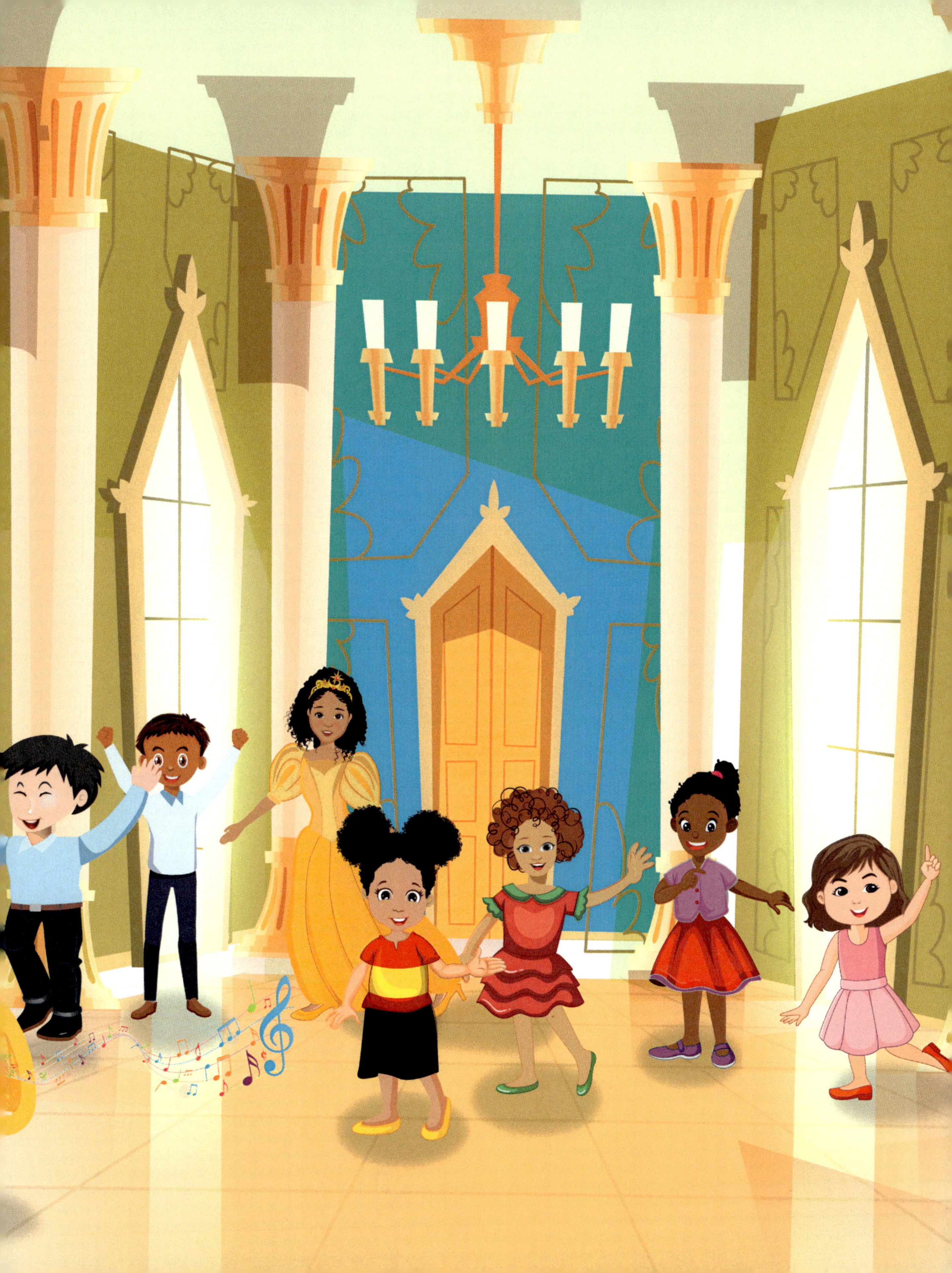

Once the guests had left the castle and Nayrobi was tucked in bed near her parents' bedroom, The queen told Nayrobi that she had seen her playing with the children in the courtyard. The children were so friendly and you were so happy. So I decided to talk to your dad about the idea of allowing the children to attend the merchant's honor party. Once I explained it to him, he agreed. "thanks mom I love you," said the Princess. The Queen said, "I love you too and oh you can begin your extra chores on Tuesday for playing in the courtyard without permission." The princess smiled saying, " ok mom, but why Tuesday?" The Queen replied because Monday you will have permission to play in the courtyard. Good night my love. Good night, mom the princess replied excitedly because now she had her parents' permission to play in the courtyard with her new friends.

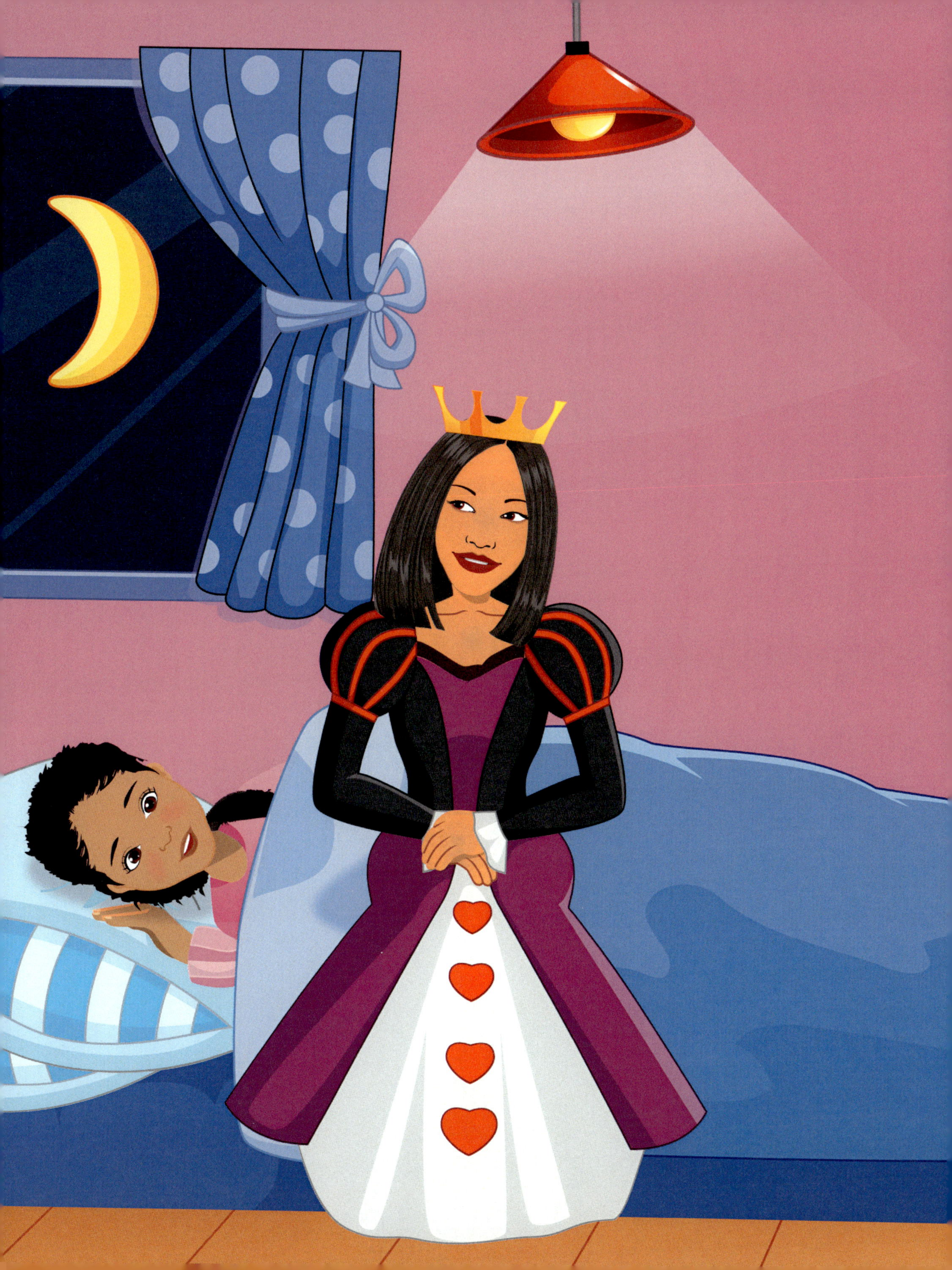

The End

Made in the USA
Middletown, DE
07 August 2024